The Strange Adventures of ROGER of WARD

by George S. Burns

Illustrated by Thomas B. Allen

Coward, McCann & Geoghegan, Inc./New York

To my father, John W. Burns
                    —GSB

To my son Ivo Allen
and our shared experiences at sea
                    —TBA

Text copyright © 1981 by George S. Burns
Illustrations copyright © 1981 by Thomas B. Allen
All rights reserved. This book, or parts thereof,
may not be reproduced in any form without permission
in writing from the publishers. Published simultaneously
in Canada by Academic Press Canada Limited, Toronto.
Library of Congress Cataloging in Publication Data
Burns, George S
   The strange adventures of Roger Ward.
   Summary: A boy goes to sea on a whaling ship and
experiences extraordinary adventures, from watching a
whale "fly" to meeting Neptune's daughter.
   [1. Fantasy. 2. Sea stories] I. Allen, Tom,
1928–   II. Title.
PZ7.B9373St   [Fic]   80-16967
ISBN 0-698-20495-6
Designed by Carolyn Craven
First printing
Printed in the United States of America

The Strange Adventures of Roger Ward

by George S. Burns
illustrated in one color by Thomas B. Allen

"In the year of our Lord 1874, while a lad of eighteen, I, Roger Ward, shipped as a raw hand aboard the whaling ship *Halo*." Tricked into signing on board by the promise that the sea air would rid him of a despised mole, Roger is an innocent young man, ignorant about the ways of the sea and its many mysteries. But as the voyage progresses, and bizarre, supernatural events keep occurring, even the old hands on the *Halo* can't explain them or predict what will happen next. This rousing story of how Roger Ward lives to tell of his extraordinary voyage is illustrated by drawings that capture the mystery and romance of a bygone era.

GEORGE S. BURNS lives in Yuba City, California.
THOMAS B. ALLEN lives in Sag Harbor, New York.

March   Ages 9-12
48 pages   7" × 10"
Fiction
$7.95, trade
(0-698-20495-6)
C, McC & G

own, the Break-of-Day Books, published
shed series of titles by talented authors
ung reader can appreciate and enjoy,
limited by a controlled vocabulary, and
ntasy to biography and history. Lively
o excite children about reading.

Fiona's Flea

BY BEVERLY KELLER

**ILLUSTRATED
IN TWO COLORS
BY DIANE PATERSON**

When Fiona finds a flea, her friends don't share
her enthusiasm for it. "How will you feel when
word gets around?" Howard scoffs. "There's no
place you can go with a flea all over—except maybe
a flea circus." Unsure of where to find a flea
circus, the unflappable Fiona goes to a flea market
for some advice. And there she finds her little
friend not only a new home, but a career! Plucky
heroine of the acclaimed *Fiona's Bee*, Fiona Foster
returns in this new story sure to gladden—and
tickle—all young lovers of unloveable animals.
Diane Paterson's drawings delightfully complement
the text's warm-hearted wit.

BEVERLY KELLER, author of *Fiona's Bee* and *Pimm's
Place*, lives in Davis, California. Diane Paterson,
illustrator of *Fiona's Bee*, lives in High Falls, New
York.

February   Ages 7-10   64 pages
5⅞" × 8½"   Fiction
$6.99, library (0-698-30719-4)

A JUNIOR LITERARY GUILD SELECTION

Coward, McCann & Geoghegan

CONTENTS

ONE · THE WHALE THAT FLEW

IN the year of our Lord 1874, while a lad of eighteen, I, Roger Ward, shipped as a raw hand aboard the whaling ship *Halo*. She was a stout three-master sailing out of Boston and by circuitous route completely around South America to the Arctic regions off Alaska. On our way to this center of the whaling grounds, we hoped to pick up a stray whale or two.

The *Halo* had barely cleared Boston Bay when I felt a twinge of sadness. I had shipped on for two years and it would be that long, or longer, before I would see my native Boston again. But the hope the salty sea air would improve my appearance gave me courage, and in a few days I had forgotten my loneliness.

I must say at this time that I am not a bad-looking young fellow, except for an ugly, purple mole on my nose. All my life I have hated that mole. The mole was a mark inflicted regularly every third generation on some member of my family. It almost broke my parents' hearts when they found out I was the one to carry this blight, but there was nothing they could do about it.

I had always been sensitive about my mole. There were times I had actually cried over it. If I saw a stranger come along the road, I would cross into a field or hide in a barn until he had passed. I couldn't stand his staring at me.

One day I overheard two sailors talking. One said to the other: "That youngster should go to sea for a few years and get rid of that mole." His companion nodded. I approached them, wondering if they could help me.

They said they would find me a berth on their ship and assured me the salty sea breeze would gradually wear off my mole. Though I longed to be an acrobat and had learned the art of tightrope walking, I made up my mind then and there to go to sea with them.

I needed my parents' consent, which they gave readily. It grieved them that I was leaving home at such an early age, but the possibility that the sea breezes might cure my mole influenced them to give their consent.

I later learned that the *Halo* needed one more sailor before it could sail that evening. I was tricked!

Nevertheless, so many strange things happened on this voyage that I had little time to reflect on my appearance, especially as we entered the Pacific Ocean and sailed along the coast of Chile, heading north now for the Aleutian Islands.

One bright morning, in latitude 20° south, just as we sighted the Bolivian coast, we were favored with a flowing wind, and with all sails spread the *Halo* sped across the blue water like a living thing. With every leap of the ship, the elevated plateaus and irregularly ridged highlands of tropical Bolivia sank lower and lower until they seemed only a few feet above sea level.

Just as land merged with horizon, a man in the crow's nest sang out that he noticed a large object to the starboard some distance away. He added excitedly that it looked like a great whale!

The *Halo* changed course to the point indicated by the lookout. A few minutes later the voice from the masthead declared positively that the object was a whale! A very large one! And it was acting in a very strange manner!

In a moment, the deck was alive with activity. Never having seen a whale, I was curious and greatly excited. As the *Halo* moved in close, the beast was identified as a sulphur whale. The sailors looked at it in astonishment. Our Captain Smith, a veteran with thirty years of whaling to his credit, gazed in speechless awe at this blue monster. The sailors stood as if grounded to the deck and stared at the fifty-foot brute with its many tons of precious blubber, oil, and bone. We watched it rise gradually to the surface. It came up very slowly, and then, just as slowly, it rose out of the water until it floated six feet in the air. It seemed that some gigantic force, a power greater than the strength of the whale, was lifting it away from its home, the sea.

And, while the beast rose higher, it snorted, puffed, and made frantic efforts to regain the water. The monster's tail was wide like the center vanes of a Dutch windmill. It beat the air with such velocity and power that it created a windstorm that rocked the *Halo* and raised waves to heights of six feet and more. Green seas washed across the deck. It was a frightening experience to feel our ship being buffeted by wind and rolling seas and to know that the cause was a whale suspended in midair. Yet the ocean outside our immediate circle was calm as a mill pond!

No one, not even our sea-wise Captain, could under-

stand any part of it. He, like the rest, could only look on, tongue-tied, wondering what in the world would come next.

Finally, the Captain found his voice. He remarked that, should the force lifting the whale continue, it would float the whale into space. But he was careful to qualify his remark by another: that he could not understand fifty tons of blubber soaring skyward. "It does not dovetail with the Law of Gravitation!" he cried.

A bright young salt, eyes bulging with excitement, suggested that the whale was in the throes of giving birth and about to become a mama. But the poor fellow wilted before the withering eye of the Captain, who asked in icy tones:

"Have you ever heard of a whale, or any other animal, becoming a mother while suspended in midair?"

This little sarcasm was cut short as just then a more awesome spectacle took place. Before our eyes the whale began to expand rapidly, like a balloon being inflated.

A hush fell upon the awe-stricken crew. The silence was so intense we could easily hear the "knock, knock" of our knees and the "tat, tat" of the sea water that went in and out of our ship's scuppers. The men's nerves were shattered, and three of them, overcome by shock, fell exhausted to the deck. Some whispered that the air was poisoned by the breath of the puffing monstrosity. They pointed at their companions stretched out on the deck as if dead. One or two of the crew cried out that it was the devil, masquerading as a whale. Others spoke up and said it was a bad omen and that the ship was under some sort of an evil spell.

The chilling sensation I experienced as all heads turned in my direction can better be imagined than described. The men were suspicious of new crew members. I had not yet gained their confidence. I held my breath as my heart pounded against my chest. I was unable to either move or speak as I gazed upon their sullen faces.

Gradually they dropped their eyes and began to discuss the unusual incident among themselves. I sighed in relief. I reasoned I was being given another chance to prove my worthiness.

While the crew talked in trembling voices, the whale expanded to more than twice its natural size. It now looked more like a small island than a whale. Five or six seagulls, which had followed our ship for days, descended from the yardarm and lighted on the monster's back.

As the whale got bigger and bigger, it gained elevation until it stood, or rather floated, twenty-five feet above the sea. The mammoth tail thrashed the air, making a churning, whirring commotion which agitated the water into a fury and shot it skyward in fountains of spray and clouds of foam.

At a height of thirty feet, the beast began to drift slowly in our direction. The men screamed that the whale was endangering the ship and our lives, but the Captain quieted their fears. He reminded us that the whale was out of its element, the sea. It was helpless, no longer able to give battle, and not to be feared. We were not so sure. The Captain added emphatically that the phenomenon we were watching had never before been witnessed by anyone. "You should note all details, remember them," he said in a strong, unafraid voice. "It will be something for

12

all of you to write home about."

"I intend," the Captain went on, "to capture that beast by lasso while it is still in the air. Anyone here with any experience in lassoing wild horses, or steers? If so, try out your skill."

Five men stepped forward, among whom were three experts in throwing the rope with unerring accuracy. They were greatly excited at the prospect of roping a whale, as indeed we all were; surely lassoing a whale in midair would be quite a remarkable event.

As the whale drifted abreast of the ship, close enough for the ropers to throw their lasso, a deathlike silence fell over the deck, and continued while the men cast their ropes. Then the crew cheered; each rope had found its mark and the beast, now quite docile, was made fast to the stern of the ship. We let out a hundred feet or more of rope so that the monster would float clear of the *Halo*.

But the crew could not imagine what the Captain would do with the whale now that it was in tow. Although the winds had stilled and there was no strain on the ship or the whale, the Captain posted two members of the crew to cut the ropes should a sudden wind come up. Meantime, we lolled upon the ocean for want of enough breeze to fill our sails.

Flocks of seagulls from the far-off shores of Bolivia circled about, then set up a loud, noisy chatter and settled on the back of the whale. Soon the surface of the beast was so crowded with the beautiful white birds that it looked like a lovely garden of white roses. But imagine a garden of white roses in the air, hanging over the Pacific Ocean!

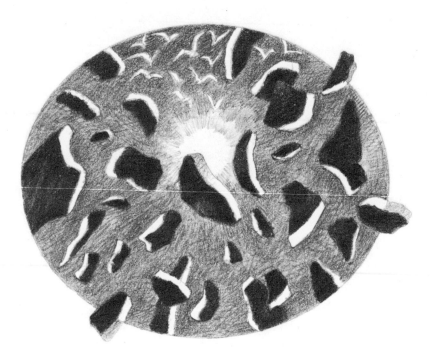

All of a sudden, the birds fell silent. Not a sign of life came from the whale. He was dead!

The gulls, having sensed it at once, crowded together, tense and alert, as if expecting something dreadful to happen. Suddenly, with whirring wing, they arose with great clamor and flew shrieking into the sky. They circled high over the *Halo*—and not a moment too soon.

Hardly had they abandoned the derelict whale than there was a deafening roar, like thunder. The bow of the *Halo* rose from the water as if lifted up by some supernatural power. I found myself hurled into space, then plunged into the sea, where I floundered.

I looked around in shock. The whale had exploded!

Aboard the *Halo,* all was confusion. So great had been the blast that two of her small boats had tumbled into the sea. Down from the sky came pellets of fat in showers, and streams of oil, warm to the touch. Then a rain of

14

tens of thousands of little fish fell upon the deck, together with chunks of blubber, weighing several hundred pounds apiece, which struck the ship fore and aft. Spars and halyards were shattered by the impact of falling whalebone. The damage was incredible.

With the help of the oil-soaked crew, I managed to scramble aboard ship. We had to wade through the monster's scattered carcass, refuse being knee-deep from stem to stern. The ship lurched and the greasy slime slithered back and forth, making it hard for the men to keep their footing on the deck.

The fish that had spewed down on us were small, hardly larger than smelts, and were clad in glittering silver skins, like armor. Biologists termed them "eulachon," but to the sailors they were "ooligans." They were the first candlelight of the Pacific coast of North America; the Indians had burned them as candles to light their underground winter homes and summer lodges before the white man came.

The Captain figured the whale had run into an enormous school of these ooligans and had gorged itself for several days, filling up beyond its natural power of digestion. The result was fermentation, which created an enormous amount of gas. This gas had caused the whale to expand to two or three times its own size, and at the same time had raised the whale out of the sea.

With the help of a couple of thousand seagulls, we managed to clean up the messy decks. Once again, the *Halo* continued on her voyage northward, cleaving the deep into flying foam and spume as the wind filled her sails.

TWO · OFF CAPE SAN LUCAS

SOME days later we came in sight of Cape San Lucas on the coast of Lower California. There we ran into a school of whales and were treated to an incredible display of water gymnastics. The whales' huge bodies, apparently buoyed by their enormous tails, bobbed up and down so fast that the motion resembled a lively dance. Around and around the whales swept in a great circle, practically standing on their tails. The sunshine flashing upon their upright bodies made them look like pillars of silver. When they came together, spray would shoot from their spouts and it seemed that they were giving each other shower baths.

Unfortunately for the whales, our business was to hunt them, not to watch their performance. After successfully harpooning two of them, we tied their dead forms to the stern of the *Halo*.

That left a third whale, who did not wish to be reduced to oil and bone, as his two playmates, now towed lifelessly astern of the *Halo,* would be. He was gigantic, having grown to the length of seventy-three feet and weighing between ninety and one hundred tons.

It was my bad luck to be a member of the boat crew

assigned to harpoon this massive mammal. My four companions were veteran harpooners and had had many en-
counters with whales, but never one so huge as this one,
nor, as we soon found out, so smart and cunning.

Jock McPherson, a Scotsman from the Barra Isles, was
in charge of the boat and the harpoon. The second in
command was Paddy Nolan, the helmsman. Paddy and
Jock were friends and always shipped together. The third
member was a young American Indian named Pasquatch.
He was the head oarsman and navigator and hailed from
Queen Charlotte Islands. The fourth and last answered to
the name of Pete. I never found out what his last name
was, or even if he had one. I, being the youngest and
surely the "greenest" of the five, bore the brunt of all
Pete's insolence.

Jock, who was an expert harpoon man, finally sank the
spear into the great beast. But it soon became apparent
that the blow was not deadly. The monster was merely
hooked. He played around for a little while as if he did
not know the harpoon was fast in his back, but he was
careful to keep out of the reach of a second thrust. He
seemed to know, if caught, he would be cut up for fer-
tilizer, his blubber turned into oil, and his whalebone
made into corsets.

The whale had been moving along swiftly for some
time and was towing us farther and farther away from
our ship. We had now lost sight of the *Halo* entirely and
began to feel ill at ease. There we were out on a vast ocean
with night coming on, in a small boat, with only half an
inch of planking between the sea and ourselves. But,
worst of all, there was no way of stopping the whale. We

could cut the rope and let him go, but he might then turn on us and with a single flip of his mighty tail and powerful flukes smash our boat into splinters and make us dinner for a shark. I was petrified.

Two of the crew got so jittery they suggested to Jock that he cut the towline anyway and try to row to a nearby shore. Jock would not hear of it, but eased our tension a little when he firmly declared, "It will get exhausted from pulling the boat. The same as the other beasts I've captured."

"Besides," he warned, "if those on the *Halo* found out we let our whale escape by cutting the towline, all of us would be scorned as cowards.

"I have never cut a towline; I always get my whale," he boasted. "And, I'll get this one, too! Anybody got anything to say about it?"

Silence followed and we looked out on the gathering darkness. The sea was calm, and we had to admit that the boat was seaworthy. Also, we were provisioned for just such an emergency. But only Jock was unafraid as we raced onward to an unknown destiny.

All through the night the great whale traveled northward at high speed, leaving in its wake a luminous track which looked eerie in the inky darkness. We sat nursing fearful thoughts, while Jock stood in the bow, ready to throw another harpoon should the whale turn around or just get tired.

The whale kept so near the shoreline that we could hear wavelets breaking on the beaches. We thought he would run himself aground or strike one of the many jutting headlands, so numerous on the coast of Lower California.

This danger was just as great for our boat. Jock called the whale a "blasted fool," but still he kept his dangerous course.

To Jock's annoyance, Paddy defended the whale's route. He figured from the whale's great size that he must be three or four hundred years old, and it was likely he had been up and down the California coast hundreds of times. The whale would not make the mistake of running aground. Said Paddy, "The brute can sense the vibration of every headland." The Scot only grunted by way of reply.

THREE · THE JACK O'LANTERNS

WE were drenched all through the night by flying spray as the whale raced on. The spray spread out in a glowing fan on either side of the boat. The whale itself, two hundred yards ahead, was also aglow and looked like a comet out in space.

Out of this fiery stream there suddenly emerged a continuous army of jack o'lanterns. They marched along the towline that was stretched between the whale boat and our mammoth steed. I watched, fascinated, as these fireflies of the ocean strutted in a fantastic procession. They would limp, bob up and down, and then sway from side to side in perfect rhythm. I could not imagine a weirder sight!

Then, hopping from the towline onto the boat, they wobbled along the gunwales. They seemed like little globes of fire and lit up our boat to such a degree that I was able to jot down the events of the day in my little diary kept dry in my waterproof pouch. Their dancing blue light gave my companions and myself a ghostly appearance. As they reached the stern of the boat, they leaped overboard and sped over the water at a terrific rate.

Soon, I discovered that these jack o'lanterns also generated a measure of heat. One of the "jacks" tripped, while wobbling along the narrow gunwale; and while trying to regain its footing, beat against my face and got hung up on the large mole on my nose. I have mentioned elsewhere how much I hated that mole and its purplish tint. As the lantern swung to and fro from my nose, it distorted my appearance and caused my companions to gasp with fright.

Then my face grew warm and, realizing the importance of my discovery, I picked up several of the larger lanterns as they came by. I felt the tingling, pleasant sensation of heat coming from each of them. Soon, although the rest of the crew was cold and wet, I felt comfortable.

This combination of light and heat made me think the lanterns might possess a measure of intelligence. I decided to try out my theory without delay.

I wrote a note on a page from my diary to our Captain on the *Halo,* telling him we were en route north along the coast much against our will; a whale had us in tow, but we were sticking with him, no matter where he might take us. I reported that the beast might be weakening and that if the *Halo* hurried there would be time to rescue us and also capture one of the largest whales afloat.

I pinned the note to the biggest jack o'lantern I could catch and instructed it to make all possible haste and deliver my message to the Captain of the *Halo.* The little fellow seemed to understand and even saluted before it sped out across the dark ocean.

Even Jock looked fearful when the whale, after a short rest, started to race again. But he was still too stubborn to cut the rope. I told no one about the note I had sent, for fear they would think I was crazy. The fact was, as time passed and no ship came to our rescue, I forgot all about the message and its will-o'-the-wisp bearer.

FOUR · A SEAGULL AND A MOLE

ON the fifth day another incident occurred. Jock and I watched a seagull light on the shaft of the harpoon in the whale's back. After resting on the shaft for a few minutes, the bird began to fly time and again into the fine spray spurting from the whale's spout. It seemed the bird was taking a shower bath, enjoying the luxury of fresh water.

Jock remarked that in his twenty years at sea he had never witnessed a similar incident; in his opinion the gull had discovered a novel way to clean itself. It was well known that fresh water would take off all the accumulation of the sea, as when a boat is put into it to remove the barnacles. Jock's explanation seemed as good as any, and we soon forgot the gull's shower bath.

The sun now beat on us with such intensity that we felt miserable and weak. It burned my mole and made it very painful. How I loathed the thing! It was Jock and Paddy that tricked me into going to sea by insisting the mole would soon disappear. They had fooled me and that was that. My mole had not worn off one bit.

Now, the mole seemed actually to attract the rays of the sun. My whole system throbbed in agony. It was as if each particle of flesh that formed the mole was on fire. To ease the pain, I tried pouring cool sea water on it, but the pain only became more severe. I did not know how much longer I could endure the agony without fainting. Then, all of a sudden, the pain left me. My nose felt strange. I put my finger up to examine it, and to my great surprise and joy, I found that the mole had disappeared. There was only a small cavity where the mole had been since I was born.

I thought the intense heat of the sun had in some way absorbed the growth. This was shared by the rest of the crew who, one by one, inspected my nose. But we were mistaken.

A few minutes later, I happened to see the mole lying at the bottom of the boat where it had fallen. It was fleshy and ugly and looked like its roots had been severed with a hot needle. I tossed it overboard.

The crew looked upon this lack of respect on my part as a bad omen. They were firm in the belief of proper burials at sea for any part of a seaman—even a mole. Now they thought my disrespect foretold bad luck. They said I should have stayed at home and joined the circus. They were angry with Jock and Paddy for having enticed me aboard the *Halo* in the first place. I sensed I was still an outsider to them and everyone wished I had gone overboard with my mole. But I was too happy that it was gone from my nose to be worried about anything—until it was announced that we had hardly a drop of water left. When that was gone, we would surely die.

FIVE · DEADLY THIRST

WE all felt on the verge of exhaustion. The last of the water had been shared among us. With the keg dry and no prospect of filling it, our situation was desperate. Our tongues grew beefy dry. We looked toward the nearby land for signs of freshness and water, but the landscape seemed a barren waste. And in separating ourselves from the whale and heading for shore we ran the risk of encountering unfriendly natives. Unarmed, and in our weakened condition, our chance of escape either by land or by sea appeared hopeless! I would have sold the whale at that moment for a glass of cold water.

While sitting in the boat thinking about the wonder of drinking water and how I had never appreciated it before, I suddenly felt giddy and heard strange sounds like voices, far, far away. I was unable to move or to speak as some uncanny power held me fast. There followed a fearful cracking and rushing of noises. The sky seemed filled with waves of dancing lights, and out of this brilliancy leaped fantastic shapes and forms, castles, strange animals of the long ago, tropical trees from which hung coconuts, bananas, and breadfruit.

So vivid and life-like were these images that flashed before me that I became almost frantic, and just before all reasoning fled my mind the force that held me began to lift. I began to stir and look around me.

Everything seemed to have changed. The sea, the boat, the whale—even the crew—looked different. My companions, who moments ago had been stretched out, half-alive, were now, to my amazement, swimming smoothly and easily around the boat and behind the whale. Then they began to dive after schools of fish and uttered cries of frustration when the fish eluded them. I stood transfixed. My confusion grew when I saw my mates with their own faces but with the bodies of seals. Desperate and weird as the situation was, I could not help but laugh as Paddy, with a woebegone look on his face, wiped a tear from his eye with one of his flippers.

When they climbed back aboard and sprawled about the boat looking precisely as they had before their transformation and their foolhardy swim, I was really confused.

The outlook was alarming. I knew we would surely die for the lack of water.

Suddenly I recalled the incident of the seagull refreshing itself in the fountain spray from the whale's spout. I was sure that the spray was indeed fresh water and, if so, the only drinkable water for miles and miles around. This is the way I reasoned:

The whale was a mammal, warm-blooded, and suckled its young like a cow on sweet, fresh milk. I was convinced that the whale was not taking in tons of salt water every day for the mere pleasure of ejecting the same water

28

through its spout. The salt in the sea water could soon clog up the vent-hole, and the whale would perish unless that vent was kept open by flushings of fresh water.

I thought the whale might be equipped with a very fine filter which instantly separated the salt from the sea water. The ejected water would be cool and fresh. I was thankful to the gull for having shown me the truth of the matter and decided to try to reach that whale, even if I lost my life in so doing. I would rather drown than die of agonizing thirst.

Gently I hinted of my plan to my thirsty companions, but only Jock heard me. The other poor fellows gave no sign of interest in anything. Jock glared at me and shook his head sadly. I gathered he thought I was going mad.

But if my companions and I were to be saved, I must act at once, regardless of Jock's displeasure. I roused the men from their stupor and made them listen.

I explained my fresh-water theory as best I could, looking all the time into unbelieving, even antagonistic, eyes. When I had finished, Jock declared that my condition was worse than any of the crew. He began to look for a coil of rope to tie me up. Pasquatch and Pete shook their heads and shrugged. Paddy, however, had a lively imagination and never took sides with Jock in any argument. He spoke up in behalf of my theory.

"I believe, Jock," said Paddy, "there is something worthwhile in the boy's theory. It sounds farfetched, but there are a great many things about whales that even the wisest know little about. For instance, no one has ever witnessed the birth of one. All of us saw the seagull fluttering about in the spray of the animal's spout. Why didn't the gull bathe in the ocean, if the water was the same?"

"The ocean don't make a fine spray like that," Jock grunted.

"Well, there's more than that," Paddy went on. "At night, the whale is lighted up by the phosphorous of the sea, and it leaves a streak of liquid fire in its wake. But the spray whirling from his vent has none of the luminescence. This means, as the boy observed, that the salt and phosphorus have in some way been eliminated from that spray. Under the light of the moon, as we have seen, the spray ejected through the vent-hole is lighted up in many colors. A rainbow forms around the whale's head. Yes, Jock, the lad is right; a rainbow is a sign of fresh water."

This reasoning seemed to stir up the crew. Their eyes brightened, and they held a private conversation for a few minutes. Then to my surprise they cried out in unison: "Water! Water! Water!"

"I tell ye, Paddy," Jock rasped, "yer all loony! It's the heat and the thirst that did it. We'll hold out for an hour or two longer. Unless we see signs of a ship by then, we'll cut the line and take our chances on the shore."

But Paddy was not to be put off. There was fire in his eyes. Jock knew better than to argue further when Paddy's temper was up.

"Come, lad," said Paddy to me. "You'll have the chance to test your theory, if you can figure out a way you can get to that whale! If you fail, we'll be no worse off than we are now. But what's worryin' me is how you're going to reach the whale."

30

"Maybe the boy can walk on water?" Jock mocked.

"No, Jock," I put in, "I'm going to walk the towrope from the boat to the whale, then board him. The distance is only a couple hundred yards. The sea is calm and there is no wind. If the whale keeps the rope taut, I can make it."

"Now, boys," Jock shook with hectic passion, "you can see for yourself that this landlubber from Massachoosetts has gone plumb crazy! The minute that whale feels a weight on the rope, he'll veer and shake it off. And not only that. If the fool lad gets there, how does he expect to keep his footing on the slick back of the whale? How does he know the whale won't dive?"

"He won't dive," I said. "It's too shallow for that. And if I feel the rope shaking, I'll hang on with hands and knees and crawl. But as long as the rope is taut, I can walk it—and in double-quick time. If I hadn't gone to sea, I'd be a tightrope walker right now. I've practiced every day since I can remember in my back yard, where I have ropes and wires of all sizes to practice on. I know there's some danger, but I think it's worth a try."

"Some danger! he says," mocked Jock. "You'll never make it. You won't go, if I have anything to say about it! I told you we'd wait."

"That ain't good enough, Jock. The rest of us are just as scared as you are that he won't make it, but as I said before, if he don't, none of us will be the worse off," said Paddy.

Jock weakened, knowing it was four against one. "If the lad wants to drown, none can say I haven't done my best to discourage him. There's the rope! There's the sea!

Ahead is the whale! Who am I to stand in his way?"

I felt elated. I stood up in the boat and took a little comb from my pocket and began to comb my long hair, pasting it back evenly as I could and parting it in the center. I didn't want even the slight weight of my hair to be off balance. A man walking a rope might be overbalanced by even an extra ounce of weight shifting suddenly to one side. I decided that, although my hob-nailed boots would make the rope-walking more difficult, they would make the boarding of the whale easier. I fastened a small bucket to my belt in which to catch the fresh water, took a small paddle for balance, shook hands with my comrades and was ready to go. Jock gave me a hearty handclasp as I stepped to the bow of the boat and a big, fatherly tear rolled down his furrowed, sun-baked face. At heart, he was a kindly man. His concern made me shiver with my first touch of fear. Maybe I couldn't make it.

SIX · MY HAIR TURNS WHITE

THE sea was oily calm; there wasn't a puff of wind. The whale was now jogging along at a slow, even rate, just enough to keep the rope taut. He appeared sleepy, but at any moment he might take a sudden notion to increase his speed. Or he might veer, or stop dead still. In any case I would be tossed into the sea and in any direction. Unless I was lucky enough to float near our boat, it might be dragged on without me. Jock would have to cut the rope to save me. He might not want to do that just to save one man and risk the lives of all the others. I was aware of the great chances I was taking, but I was also aware that, if I did not take them, we were doomed to die of thirst.

Jock and Paddy helped me out of the boat and onto the running line. My legs were stiff from sitting so long in the same position, and it was difficult for me to adjust my feet to the rope because of the boots I was wearing. Cautiously, I took a few short steps forward. At first, my pace was snail-like; I had to accustom myself to the sensation of the sea below me and test my strength. But soon I was able to balance myself firmly.

The towline was only two-thirds of an inch in thickness, and for some way out it was two inches below the surface of the water. Fortunately the water magnified the rope somewhat and it was quite visible.

Without the paddle, it would have been impossible for me to have made any headway. I had cut a groove in the paddle and, by sliding it along the line, I got all the support I needed and kept my balance. At short intervals I would rest on the paddle and take long breaths, filling my lungs with the stimulating California air, which was scented with sagebrush.

The whale gave no sign he was aware of my movement. I thanked Neptune, or whatever sea-god there was who cared for my welfare, for guiding that whale steadily forward. Suddenly, a vagrant seagull landed on my head. I staggered under the impact. The gull drove its sharp claws through my felt hat and deep into my flesh, causing blood to run down my face and drip off my stubbled chin.

I went off my head with terror. My hair stood upright, lifting both my hat and the gull, which flew off. I looked down into the glassy water and could see in my reflection my hair gradually change color, from black to white. My nerves were pretty well shattered, and I went on by sheer instinct.

SEVEN · THE SEA GODDESS

WHEN within a hundred feet or so of the whale, I suddenly saw an object on the back of the monster, something alive and walking about. It was much too big for a bird of any kind, and so far as I knew only birds, or perhaps pilot fish, would ride a whale. Cautiously, I moved ahead.

The glare of the sun and the bright shimmering sea had so dazzled my eyes that I thought I was seeing a human form. As I neared the whale's tail, I realized that it was indeed a person—one of those creatures I had heard the crew discussing on occasions, though no one had ever seen one. This was a young woman—a goddess.

I was filled with wonder. The girl's garments shone with a dazzling white luster. She seemed to be wrapped in cloth spun from a sunbeam. Her golden hair was bound up and piled on top of her head in graceful swirls, and her face was refined and of rare beauty.

So overwhelming was her loveliness that I might have fallen into the sea and perished had the lovely creature not called to me in a sweet voice to have courage and board the whale. She stretched forth her hand and smiled. I blushed so deeply the glow singed my ear.

Boarding a whale is risky; I would not advise it as a sport. The skin is as slippery as soap suds, because of its own sliminess and because it is partly submerged in water. Also, one has to contend with the animal's rolling motion as it propels itself through the sea. And here was a beautiful girl coming to my assistance, and making my efforts seem foolish. I was flustered and a little annoyed at being seen in my awkwardness.

To help me up, she loosened and then braided her long, flowing hair into a soft but strong rope and tossed me the end of it. Then, with a firm tread of her tiny bare feet, she slowly moved up the mountainous side of the whale. I held on and followed her until I was safely on the monster's back. There, I bowed to her and kissed the golden tress I held in my hand. The courtesy seemed to delight her.

As I stood up on the back of the whale, I could hear the crew's hearty cheer. They were waving their hats energetically. I raised my paddle in acknowledgment.

I knew my appearance pleased her, for the girl smiled on me. My, what a heavenly smile that was! In her left cheek was a beautiful dimple as deep as the eye in an Irish potato. She introduced herself, and I was flabbergasted when she told me she was Aristone, twenty-seventh daughter of Neptune and Goddess of the Deep. She was next in command of the great oceans that circled the globe, under her father, the great Neptune. At her birth she was given great powers over the animals and fish of all oceans.

She had had several misunderstandings with her father, she said. He did not approve of many things she did. She liked to play hide and seek with mermen among the coral reefs and underwater caverns. She had to her credit the discovery of several lost cities which had sunk long ago to the bottom of the sea. Many of these cities were still intact, and she liked to go and explore them, without Neptune's permission. Her independence would make her father angry, and when he lost his temper it would bring about terrific storms at sea—every time he waved his arms and shouted at her, gigantic waves frothed and rolled landward, pulling rocks from their ancient foundations and changing the contour of the coast wherever they struck. Realizing the damage Neptune's temper caused, Aristone always did her best to make him calm once more.

As she told me all this, I studied her dress, which appeared different up close. I had been mistaken in the nature of the material, which I had thought was cloth of various shades; now I saw she wore an elaborate veiling of sea water. Drops overlapped each other like shingles on the roof of a house, except that there were millions of them, all so tiny they appeared as one sheet of gauzy lace. Stranger still, these drops hung together and glowed and shimmered in the sunshine, not solidly, but in constant motion, moving in circles around the goddess. This motion, I noticed, occurred only in that part of the dress below the graceful waistline. The skirt was bordered by a narrow band of ocean foam, like the thin white streak of some happy wavelet as it dances against the shimmering shoreline on a golden beach.

The whole dress was semitransparent, so I could not help but see she had lovely ankles, and still lovelier legs.

Indeed she was a goddess—a perfect goddess—if there ever was one.

After a while, she became sad and thoughtful and had ceased to be aware of my presence. I noticed her skirt begin to drip onto the whale's back. First, the white strip of foam around the fringe melted away, then so did row upon row of the salt water drops that made up the rest of the garment, until her charming ankles were bare.

I stood aghast as the shimmering drops went on falling, exposing her alabaster limbs inch by inch. I felt so embarrassed and blushed so deeply that the few hairs on my chin shriveled and disappeared. Unless I acted promptly her entire costume would vanish.

I took the liberty of tapping her, ever so gently, upon the shoulder. She gave a little start, but smiled beamingly upon me—it was such an innocent smile. I pointed to her rapidly diminishing dress. She saw my concern and snapped back from her distractions. The dripping ceased, and then at her command hundreds of little drops arose to renew the shape of the lovely garment. Mounting from the sea, they one by one attached themselves to one another, until the dress was again complete. Then a tiny wave flung itself to the edge of her skirt, and behold: Aristone stood in all her loveliness, just as before!

Needless to say, I stood amazed at all these strange happenings on the back of a whale, and right before my very eyes!

Aristone had the softest and most musical voice imaginable; it made me forget my troubles and gave me a feeling of great peace. But that was not all. Every time she spoke, the sea around the whale vibrated and bubbled

up in little gushing fountains. The water somehow re-
sponded to the melody of her voice, and could not help
but dance to it. I wanted to dance too—but I heard the
faint, breeze-borne voices of my comrades, calling "Water!
Water!" and I remembered I had a job to do.

EIGHT · WATER! WATER! WATER!

AFTER their long immersion in the water, my feet felt stiff and numb. To limber up I walked around on the back of the whale, an area of about five hundred square feet, far greater than many a large garden plot. Aristone kept me steady by holding my arm. I wondered how she could walk so well in bare feet until I saw that they barely touched the whale. It looked as if she were walking on air.

While walking with the daughter of Neptune, I told her my reason for boarding the whale. After hearing my pitiful tale and learning about the distress of my four comrades, she grew agitated. Instantly, she unslung my little pail and went toward the spray scattering from the whale's spout. Expertly she caught the water in the bucket, and in a few minutes, it was filled to overflowing. She came to me and held the pail to my parched lips.

I drank deeply. It was the most refreshing drink I had ever tasted! My theory was right about the seagull; here, indeed, was fresh water from the fountain of the whale.

After drinking long drafts of sweet water, I felt new vigor stir within me. I thanked the goddess for her kindness and told her that I now felt strong enough to haul in the boat by the towline, so that my thirsty comrades might also have water.

Aristone stood erect and stretched forth her hand toward the boat. To my amazement, the boat instantly began to leap over the water toward the whale, and as it did the towline coiled itself of its own accord into the stern. The men were astonished. They may have been so tired that they thought they were dreaming the entire thing. Of course, they were unaware of Aristone, who had brought about this phenomenon, for she had only revealed herself to me. She whispered to me her fear was that if they saw something else besides myself moving about, they might panic and harm themselves.

When the crew reached the whale, I passed Jock the bucket and told him to hand up another pail which I could fill while they shared the contents of the first one. But the goddess, seeing their real distress, now concentrated the entire spray into a long stream and directed it over the length of the boat from bow to stern, so the poor fellows could drink from the stream without delay. All the while the goddess was studying the men. Could this have been her first view of human beings?

Not having washed at all for many days, my mates looked wild and dirty. Aristone suspended the spray over the boat so they could clean themselves and refill the water keg. This they did, greatly enjoying the cool freshness of the precious water.

Though the water quenched our thirst, it could not ease our hunger. Aristone was surprised. She was unaware of the need humans had for food. Her only requirements were the soft morning breezes and the delicate threads of

44

sunlight. However, after a thoughtful moment, she added: "If the men are hungry, they must be fed. Tell them to get prepared and they will eat shortly."

The men had no more than drawn their knives when platters of food appeared before them. And delightful food it was, tasty and exotic. There were slices of beef, cubed lamb, crab meat, smoked salmon with little rice cakes. Other platters were laden with quantities of cheese, bowls of milk, ripe grapes, and flaky honey pastry. The starving men wolfed down the food and, after a bit, began to return to their old selves. They waved their caps and shouted my name. I felt quite a hero.

Aristone was so touched by the recovery of the crew that a big tear rolled down her cheek—and a wonderful tear it was. As it fell upon the whale's back, it turned into a sparkling diamond! Aristone motioned to me to put it in my pocket. I thought it might melt, but it didn't. It was a real diamond of great value, which I could keep always!

Aristone saw how tired I was, and suggested I return to my place on the boat and rest. I thought it odd my crewmates did not help me—they sat there motionless, as if in a trance. Aristone paid them no heed as she guided me.

"I'll make a pillow for your white head," she said, with an enchanting smile. No sooner had she spoken than the whispering zephyrs that were playing about the surface of the water came together, and with her own dainty hands she gathered them into a wonderful pillow—softer than feathers and cool as a spring wind. Then, from the flowing silver of the streaming sun, she made a comforter, lighter than thistledown, which she spread over me. It was silvery in color, warm and cozy, its borders trimmed in yellow. It was a mystery to me how she gathered the stuff from the air, but she did, and she tucked me into this magnificent wrap, which was so comfortable I fell into a restful sleep almost immediately. But just before I dropped off, I said to Aristone, "Do you think I am an old man because I have white hair?"

"Oh, no!" she smiled. "I watched it change. I was just thinking, I like black hair better."

"So do I," I told her. Then my eyes shut and I was asleep.

I must have slept for many hours—all through the night in fact. When I awoke the sun was high above the horizon, and Aristone was gone!

The whale, too, had gone. It was nowhere to be seen. My excited companions told me that during the early morning hours the whale had suddenly quickened its speed. With a mighty surge that snapped the towline, it headed toward the open sea and was not seen again.

The crew was disappointed and angry about the loss of the whale. I could not fault them for their bitterness. In their attempt to capture it, they suffered many hardships.

Secretly, I was pleased it had escaped. He was a noble beast—a worthy adversary—and besides, without him, I may never have met Aristone or rid myself of that horrible mole.

Suddenly, Jock shouted that before us was Point Lobos, some twenty miles south of Monterey. We were safe!

My companions beached the boat and made a fire as I stripped off my clothes and plunged into the sea. I hoped that Aristone might reappear, but she did not, and I was never to see her again.

However, she did leave two mementos. One was a magnificent diamond, worth a king's ransom—and the other, my naturally black hair.

My companions never did mention the fresh water from the whale's spout or the food that saved our lives. When I spoke of Aristone they would turn from me and look to one another. I wondered at their indifference and was about to scold them for their ingratitude when a ship appeared on the horizon. To our joy, it was the *Halo,* which immediately put out small boats for us.